A Present For Pig

by Elli Woollard

Illustrated by Al Murphy

ff

FABER & FABER

In the faraway village of
Snottington Sneeze
Woozy the wizard whizzed
fast through the trees.

And there on his broomstick
right at the end,
Sat his little pet **Pig**,
his very best friend.

But one sunny Saturday

Woozy woke up

And he poured out some tea

(Just forgetting the cup).

Then he looked at his Pig

and he said to her, 'Now,

I know today's **special**;

I just can't think how.'

What could it be?

Woozy thought and he thought,

Till his precious pet Pig

gave a cross sort of snort.

'Pig?' Woozy said.

'What's the matter? And why

Are you wearing a **tutu**

and sparkly bow tie?'

But just before Woozy

could think any more

There came a loud

rat-a-tat-tat at his door . . .

And the postman was there,

holding whole hills of things

Such as letters and packets

and parcels with strings.

'Pig's birthday?' cried Woozy.

'How **could** I forget!

I've not got a present

or card for her yet!'

PIG
PIG
PIG

'I need something quickly.

I need to be swift.

Pig mustn't guess that

I've not got a gift.'

Woozy searched round his house

in the crannies and nooks

Among potions and lotions

and spell-making books.

OLD JUNK

He found some old hankies,

some small and some big,

But he didn't think those were

a good gift for Pig.

What, Woozy thought,

would my Pig like to get?

I'll ask my friend Dripsy –

she'll know it, I bet.

So he got on his broom

and he **zoomed** through the air

Till he came to a draughty

and dragonish lair.

'Dripsy!' said Woozy.

'Your brain is so big;

Do you think you could think up

a gift for my Pig?'

'That's easy!' said Dripsy.

'I know it already!

Some sort of toy

like a train or a teddy.'

Woozy went home,

where he saw some balloons,

And his Pig humming sad

happy-birthday-ish tunes.

I'll just say a spell,

Woozy thought, then **ta-dah!**

A toy for my Pig,

who's my best friend by far!

He took out his wand and cried,

'Abraca-power!'

But all that he got was a . . .

. . . shower of flour!
FLOUR

'Oh **bother!'** said Woozy

'I need to be swift!

Pig mustn't guess that

I've not got a gift.

But what can I do?'

Woozy said to himself.

'I think that I'll go and ask

Iffy the elf!'

'Bye Pig!' said Woozy.

'I'll just be a jiffy!'

He got on his broom

and **zipped** off to find Iffy,

Who lived in a hole

at the top of a hill,

Where Woozy's nose **froze**

in the frost and the chill.

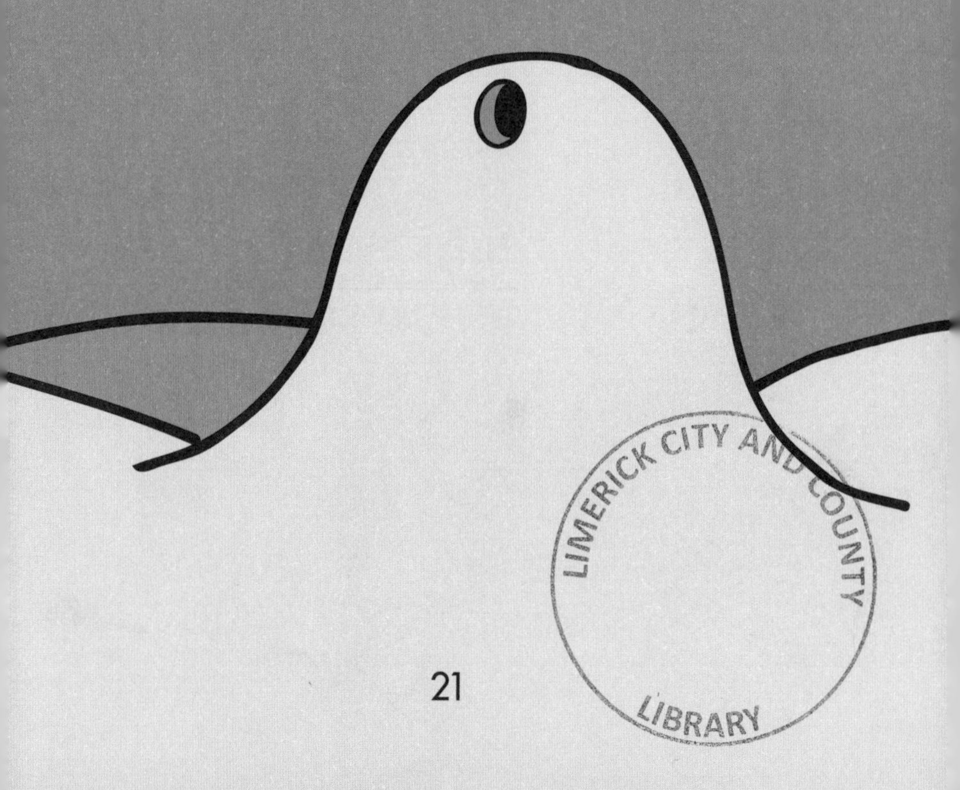

'Iffy!' said Woozy.

'Your brain is so **big**;

Do you think you could think up

a gift for my Pig?'

'A doddle!' said Iffy.

'Just get Pig a bike!

She's sure to ride stylishly!

That's what she'd like!'

Woozy got home

and he opened the door,

And there was his Pig

with a badge that said '4'.

I'll just say a spell,

Woozy thought, then ta-dah!

A bike for my Pig,

who's my best friend by far!

He took out his wand and cried,

'Abraca-sunny!'

But all that he got was . . .

. . . some bees

(and some honey).

'Oh **bother!'** said Woozy.

'I need to be swift!

Pig mustn't guess that

I've not got a gift.

But what can I do?

I've got nothing at all!

I know, I'll visit

Witch Titch and Witch Tall.'

The witches both lived in

the deep creepy wood.

Woozy went in.

It did NOT feel too good.

There were small crawling creatures

with huge hungry eyes,

And things that made Woozy say,

'Oo!' in surprise.

'Witches!' said Woozy.
'Your brains are so big;
Do you think you could think up
a gift for my Pig?'

'No problem!' Witch Titch said.
'Just get Pig a drum
Or a rock-star guitar with some
strings she can strum.'

Woozy went home,

where his Pig (in a crown)

Gave Woozy a

down-in-the-dumps

sort of frown.

I'll just say a spell,

Woozy thought, then **ta-dah!**

A drum for my Pig,

who's my best friend by far!

He took out his wand and cried,

'Abraca-peg!'

But all that he got was a . . .

. . . freshly-laid egg!

'Oh **bother!'** said Woozy.

'This just isn't fair!'

And he looked for his Pig,

but his Pig wasn't there!

Woozy searched everywhere,

round and about.

'Pig, are you hiding?'

he said. **'Please** come out!'

But all that he found

was some tall pointy hats,

Some spell books and spiders

and twenty black bats.

'Oh dear!' Woozy said.

'Is my Pig feeling miffed?

Maybe she's guessed

that I've not got a gift.

My spells are **disastrous!**

They just make a mess!'

Then Woozy said,

'Hmm, I should tidy, I guess.

This egg and the flour

and the honey are trash.'

So he threw them away

with a clatter

clunk

crash!

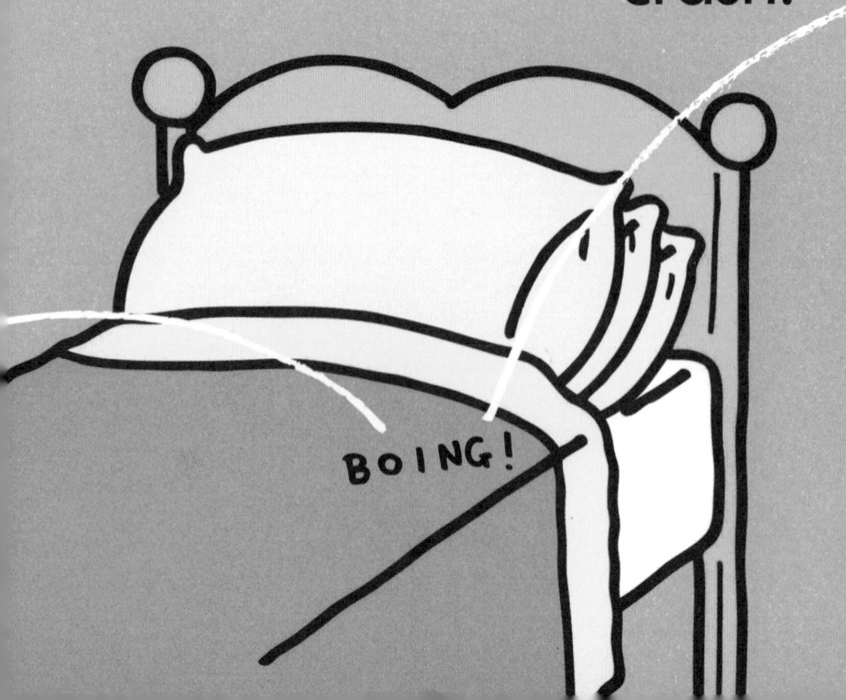

But they all missed the bin,

then bounced off the bed,

And ended up . . .

. . . splat!

in the cauldron instead.

'And now,' Woozy said,

'since my spells are a flop

I will go out and buy Pig

a gift from the shop.'

The silly old wizard

was not even looking

So didn't once spot

that his rubbish was . . .

. . . cooking.

The egg, flour and honey

(and also some oil)

Had started to glimmer

and simmer and boil.

Nobody stirred it;

the pot was untroubled,

As sizzling and frizzling

it blissfully bubbled.

Woozy went to the shops,

but he just found a rose,

Four candles, whipped cream

and some big silky bows.

'Oh dear!' Woozy said.

'That is not a good gift.'

Then all of a sudden,

he stopped, and he sniffed.

'Mmmm,' Woozy said.

'Such a marvellous smell!

What is it, I wonder?

I can't really tell.'

But as he stood wondering

what it could be.

He heard someone shouting,

'Hey Woozy! Coo-ee!'

It was Dripsy, the Witches

and Iffy the elf!

'Why are they here?'

Woozy said to himself.

'We've come for Pig's party,'

said Titch. 'Are we late?

Whatever you're cooking,

it smells really great!'

'A party?' said Woozy.

'Oh no! Dearie me!

I've not got a present,

or food for the tea!'

'Are you sure?' Iffy said.

'Did we make a mistake?

It's just that this smell

smells a lot like a . . .

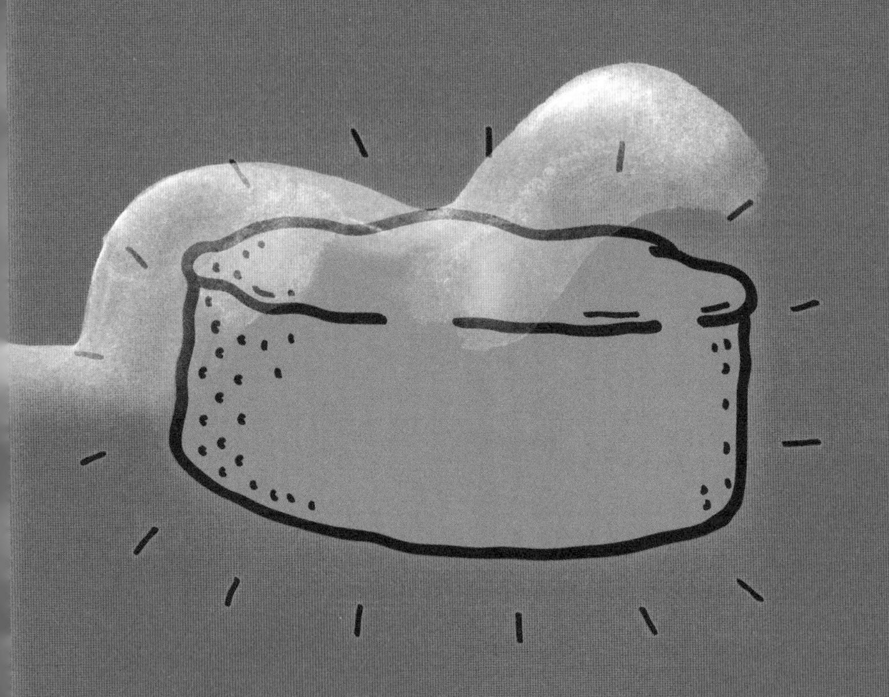

. . . cake!'

And Woozy just stood there

and tugged at his beard,

Saying, 'How did this get here?

It's all very weird.'

'A cake by mistake!'

said the witches. 'Oh wow!'

And Dripsy said, 'Yes!

Let the party start NOW!'

'But wait,' Woozy said,

'we can't simply start snacking.

There's something not right here;

there's something that's lacking.'

I know what's missing:

it's Pig! Woozy thought,

When he suddenly heard

the most pleased sort of snort.

Pig grinned, then she lifted

her snout and she sniffed,

And everyone said,

'This big cake's a GREAT gift!'

'Hang on!' Woozy said.

'It needs candles as well.

Look what I bought!

See, I don't need a spell.'

And he put on the candles

and also the rose,

Some squirts of whipped cream

and the big silky bows.

Then Dripsy breathed flames

(rather fearsome and big).

'Hooray!' Woozy said,

'HAPPY BIRTHDAY, dear Pig!'

Then everyone gave Pig

a present and card,

And the cake tasted good,

if a tiny bit charred.

A P[illegible]esent For Pig

For Jack & Charley
A. M.

First published in 2016
by Faber and Faber Limited
Bloomsbury House
74–77 Great Russell Street
London WC1B 3DA

Designed by Faber and Faber
Printed in China

A CIP record for this book is available from the British Library

978–0571–31319-8

2 4 6 8 10 9 7 5 3 1